Childhood Trauma

Other titles in the *Emerging Issues in Public Health* series include:

Cell Phone Addiction

Gun Violence

Lead Contamination

The Opioid Crisis

EMERGING ISSUES IN PUBLIC HEALTH

Childhood Trauma

Peggy J. Parks

ReferencePoint Press

San Diego, CA

ReferencePoint Press®

Printed in the United States

For more information, contact:
ReferencePoint Press, Inc.
PO Box 27779
San Diego, CA 92198
www.ReferencePointPress.com

LIBRARY OF CONGRESS CATALOGING-IN-PUBLICATION DATA

Name: Parks, Peggy J., 1951– author.
Title: Childhood Trauma/by Peggy J. Parks.
Description: San Diego, CA: ReferencePoint Press, Inc., 2020. | Series: Emerging Issues in Public Health | Audience: Grade 9 to 12. | Includes bibliographical references and index.
Identifiers: LCCN 2019014173 (print) | LCCN 2019015325 (ebook) | ISBN 9781682826683 (eBook) | ISBN 9781682826676 (hardback)
Subjects: LCSH: Psychic trauma in children—Juvenile literature.
Classification: LCC RJ506.P66 (ebook) | LCC RJ506.P66 P37 2020 (print) | DDC 618.92/8521—dc23
LC record available at https://lccn.loc.gov/2019014173

CONTENTS

Traumatized

A New York City girl named Nadia had an extremely troubled life. Her father repeatedly abused her, and her mother was an addict who was often high on drugs. After Nadia's teachers reported that she was being abused and neglected, she was removed from her home and placed in foster care. Yet her young life remained in turmoil because she was bounced around from one foster home to another. This, along with what she had gone through with her parents, took a heavy toll on Nadia's mental and physical health. She often felt sad, lonely, and anxious about what would happen to her. While living in foster homes, she worried constantly about her siblings, which kept her awake night after night. The lack of sleep worsened her anxiety, and she began to act out, lying and stealing clothing, food, and other items. When she was punished for these wrongdoings, she felt even more isolated and alone.

Such distressing and emotionally painful experiences are known as traumas. Research has shown that an alarming number of children and adolescents are affected by trauma every year—and they are often traumatized in more than one way. As a result, medical professionals and health officials continue to grow increasingly concerned about this issue. In a February 2017 article, New York City psychologist and trauma specialist Matthew Oransky writes, "Trauma is our nation's unspoken public health crisis."[1]

Alarming Statistics

Mental health professionals often use the term *adverse childhood experiences*, or *ACEs*, to describe childhood trauma. This term applies to many different kinds of incidents, all of which can be traumatic for young people. As in Nadia's case, physical and emotional abuse and neglect are examples of ACEs, as is living with a parent who is addicted to drugs or alcohol. Other sources of childhood trauma range from the loss of a parent through divorce, death, or incarceration to witnessing acts of violence or being affected by a natural disaster.

> "Trauma is our nation's unspoken public health crisis."[1]
>
> —Matthew Oransky, a psychologist from New York City who specializes in trauma

Childhood trauma was the subject of a comprehensive study released by the Health Resources & Services Administration in October 2017. The final report revealed how serious and widespread ACEs are throughout the United States. The researchers found that more than 46 percent of children and adolescents—34 million—have experienced one or more types of trauma, and nearly 22 percent have experienced two or more. Those with multiple childhood traumas have the highest risk of developing mental and/or physical health problems. "The

Children can be traumatized when they live with parents or guardians who are addicted to drugs or alcohol.

higher your ACE score, the worse your health outcomes,"[2] says pediatrician Nadine Burke Harris, who is California's surgeon general.

Trauma: Devastating to the Body and Mind

The health problems that occur because of childhood trauma are rooted in hormones. When someone is traumatized, the brain is flooded with stress hormones such as cortisol and adrenaline. Under normal conditions these hormones play a crucial role in what is called the fight-or-flight response, which is a natural reaction that occurs whenever people feel threatened or afraid. A surge of stress hormones is released by the adrenal glands located atop the kidneys, causing the heart rate to speed up, blood pressure to spike, and other bodily changes to occur that prepare someone to either stay and fight off the threat or run away from it.

The fight-or-flight response is critical for human survival; without it, people would not be able to sense or combat threats or danger. But when stress is constant, the stress response does not turn off as it should, which results in excessive levels of stress hormones. Julian Ford, a psychiatry professor and director of the Center for Trauma Recovery and Juvenile Justice at UConn Health, explains, "Kids who've experienced trauma can be stuck in permanent survival mode—hyper-vigilant and constantly on edge—waiting for the next awful thing to happen. Kids often don't realize or understand why they're reacting the way they do."[3]

Such prolonged periods of stress, often called toxic stress, can increase a trauma sufferer's risk of depression, severe anxiety, and post-traumatic stress disorder. It has also been associated with drug and alcohol abuse. According to Oransky, at least 70 percent of adolescents in substance abuse treatment programs have a history of trauma exposure. Also, trauma vastly increases the risk of suicide, which is the second leading cause of death for teens aged fifteen to nineteen.

Yet the effects of childhood trauma are not limited to young people. As a result of trauma experienced as children, many adults suffer from health problems later in life. Scientists have linked a history of trauma with high blood pressure, elevated cholesterol levels, and increased risk of type 2 diabetes. Other diseases that research has linked to ACEs include arthritis, gastrointestinal disease, heart conditions, migraine headaches, and sleep disturbances.

The strong connection between physical and mental health problems among adults and the trauma they experienced during childhood was confirmed in a major study published in November 2018. Adult participants with histories of trauma were 1.5 times more likely to suffer from psychiatric disorders than adults whose childhoods were not affected by trauma. Participants with traumatic childhoods also had a higher-than-normal risk of developing poor overall health, participating in risky behaviors, struggling financially, and/or being involved in violent relationships.

> "Adverse childhood experiences are the single greatest unaddressed public health threat facing our nation today."[4]
>
> —Robert Block, a pediatrician and former president of the American Academy of Pediatrics

A Growing Sense of Urgency

The November 2018 study confirmed what researchers have long believed: that there is a definitive link between psychiatric and physical problems in adults and the trauma they experienced as children. This, along with the growing awareness of the prevalence of childhood trauma, is leading to its recognition as one of America's most pressing issues. As former American Academy of Pediatrics president Robert Block explains, "Adverse childhood experiences are the single greatest unaddressed public health threat facing our nation today."[4]

A Public Health Emergency

Since the mid-1990s, when the first major study of childhood trauma was published, scientists have compiled a vast amount of research on the topic. This has broadened scientific understanding of its causes, its effects on children and adolescents, and its prevalence, including the regions of the United States where it is most prevalent. Although much remains unknown, scientists and health officials widely agree that childhood trauma is one of society's most urgent problems.

One report that highlighted this urgency was released in February 2018 by Child Trends, an organization that conducts research on improving children's lives. Using a comprehensive analysis of data from a national children's health survey, researchers found that nearly half of children and youth in the United States have experienced at least one ACE, and many experienced more than one. "There's an increasing awareness that these experiences are a really important public-health issue,"[5] says Child Trends research scientist Vanessa Sacks.

The Many Causes of Trauma

Although children can be, and are, subjected to a disturbing variety of traumatic experiences, such experiences have proved to be much more common than others. According to the Child Trends report, the most prevalent ACE, affecting an average of 25.5 percent of children, is living in a family that does not have enough income to pay for basic expenses like food and housing. That ACE is closely followed by divorce of parents or guardians, which affects about 25 percent of children.

The next most common source of trauma, affecting 9 percent of children, is living in a family in which someone has a drug or alcohol problem. An estimated 8.2 percent of children have been traumatized due to a parent or guardian being incarcerated, and 7.8 percent live with someone who is mentally ill, suicidal, or severely depressed. Other ACEs cited in the Child Trends report include seeing or hearing parents or other adults acting violently in the home (5.7 percent), being the victim of or witnessing neighborhood violence (3.9 percent), often being treated unfairly or judged due to race or ethnicity (3.7 percent), and the death of a parent or guardian (3.3 percent).

Aside from the traumatic incidents that affect young people most frequently, trauma can also result from a number of other experiences. Being physically, emotionally, or sexually abused, for example, is among the worst trauma a child or adolescent can endure. Neglect is also traumatic; some experts, in fact, say it is even more traumatic than abuse because children need so desperately to feel loved and accepted. Other potential sources of trauma include experiencing violence at school, such as a shooting; bullying; living in a home where there is domestic violence; being affected by a devastating fire or natural disaster; and/or being involved in a serious automobile accident.

A Teacher's Disturbing Discovery

As awareness of childhood trauma has grown over the years, professionals who work with children and adolescents have become more concerned about its prevalence. This is true of Bill Soules, a psychology teacher from New Mexico. Soules was familiar with childhood trauma, having studied the research, and he knew about the close connection between ACEs and mental and physical illness. After reading about the soaring prevalence of ACEs, Soules decided that childhood trauma would be a good discussion topic for his advanced placement (AP) psychology classes. He developed a ten-question survey and gave each student a blank note card to anonymously record any ACEs he or she had experienced.

Traumatic Events Experienced by US Youth

According to the National Survey of Children's Health, nearly half of the nation's young people experienced at least one of nine traumatic events in 2016 (the most current year for which these statistics are available). This supports the view of many experts—that childhood trauma has become a public health crisis. The graph shows the percentage of young people from birth through age seventeen who experienced at least one of the listed traumatic events. Researchers call these events adverse childhood experiences, or ACEs.

Most Prevalent Traumatic Experiences for Children and Adolescents

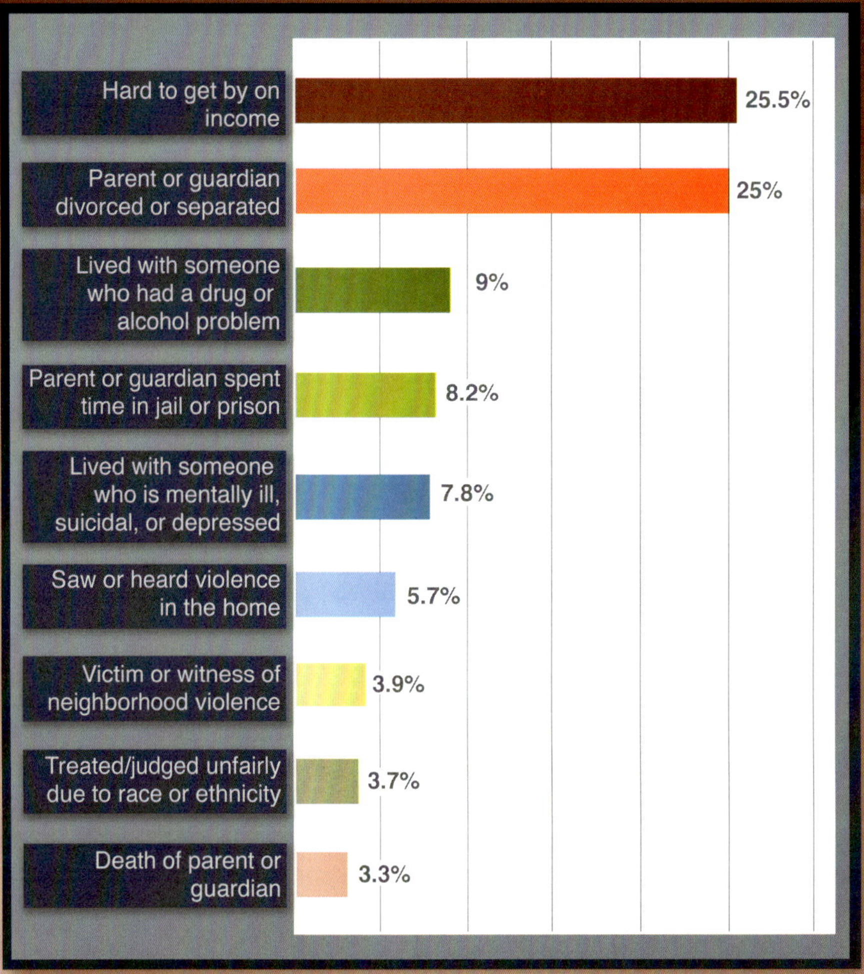

Source: C.D. Bethell et al., "Adverse Childhood Experiences Among US Children," Child & Adolescent Health Measurement Initiative, Johns Hopkins Bloomberg School of Public Health, October 2017. www.cahmi.org.

When Soules collected the cards and reviewed the results, he was stunned. Out of thirty-four students in one class, twenty-two reported three or more ACEs, and twelve had six or more. "Way higher than what I expected or what the national averages indicate,"[6] he says. He was equally taken aback at the results from his second class. Again, twenty-two students had three or more ACEs, and four had eight or more. This led to an open and honest discussion about the students' lives, with one girl saying that people see her only as an excellent student who takes AP classes but really know nothing about her. Soules heard one heart-wrenching story after another. "I tried to listen and let them talk while I was on the edge of tears as they told their stories," he says. "I couldn't help thinking, *and these are the AP students who are doing well. How many other students are there who are not feeling any success?*"[7]

By far, says Soules, the most common question from the students after this exercise was why society has allowed childhood trauma to become such a serious, widespread problem. "They are right," he says. "We need to do something about the trauma our children are experiencing. . . . It is a public health issue. It is a moral issue. We need to pull back the curtain and deal with this crisis in an open way."[8]

Geographical Variations

Although traumatic experiences affect children and adolescents in every US state, studies have revealed differences based on where they live. Child Trends researchers found that Arkansas has the most cases of childhood trauma, with 56 percent of children experiencing at least one traumatic incident during 2016. The lowest number of ACEs was in Minnesota, where 37 percent of children experienced at least one during 2016.

Research has also detected regional differences in the children who have endured multiple traumatic incidents—and unsurprisingly, those children's risk for negative health outcomes is significantly higher than children with one ACE. As Sacks and her

> "The accumulation of ACEs, rather than any particular ACE, is most strongly predictive of negative outcomes."[9]
>
> —Vanessa Sacks and David Murphey, research scientists with Child Trends

colleague David Murphey explain, "The accumulation of ACEs, rather than any particular ACE, is most strongly predictive of negative outcomes."[9]

On a national level, one in ten children (10 percent) have experienced three to eight ACEs. In five states—Arizona, Arkansas, Montana, New Mexico, and Ohio—as many as one in seven children (14.3 percent) have experienced three to eight ACEs. Other states with high numbers of children with multiple ACEs include Idaho, Kentucky, Louisiana, Maine, Mississippi, and West Virginia. Although researchers cannot say for sure why such profound differences exist, they strongly suspect that poverty is a factor. According to the Children's Defense Fund, Arkansas, New Mexico, Kentucky, Louisiana, Mississippi, and West Virginia have some of the country's highest rates of extreme childhood poverty, and those states also have extraordinarily high numbers of children who have endured multiple traumatic incidents.

Racial Disparities

Along with state-by-state differences, race is a strong indicator of which children most often experience trauma. "In almost every group of states we looked at, as well as nationally, white and Asian children have the lowest rates of ACEs, while black and Hispanic children tend to have the highest,"[10] says Sacks. During their research, she and Murphey found that 61 percent of black children and 51 percent of Hispanic children have experienced one or more ACEs, compared with 40 percent of white children and 23 percent of Asian children.

Although living in poverty and experiencing the divorce of a parent or guardian are the most common ACEs for all children, regardless of race, other types of trauma differ according to race. Among white children, for example, the next most common ACEs

Although ACEs affect children of all races, research has shown that black children are affected far more than Hispanic, white, and Asian children.

are living with someone who has a substance abuse problem, followed by living with someone who is mentally ill, suicidal, or severely depressed. For Hispanic children, the next most common ACEs are living with someone who has a substance abuse problem, followed by having an incarcerated parent. Among black children, experiencing the death of a parent or guardian is among the most common ACEs, as is living in a family in which there is domestic abuse. Also, black children are more than twice as likely as white children to have a parent who is incarcerated.

When a Parent Goes to Prison

Other studies show parental incarceration is even more prevalent among Hispanic and black children. According to a February 2018 report by the public health group Human Impact Partners, black children are nine times more likely than white children to have a parent in prison, and Hispanic children are three times more likely. Losing a parent to incarceration can be extremely traumatic for young people, as criminal justice advocate Renee Menart writes: "Whether a child's parent is currently or previously incarcerated, the implications are long-lasting and life-altering. Children with adverse childhood experiences, including a parent's incarceration, may face mental health challenges that continue well into adulthood."[11]

Anyé Young is a teenager who knows firsthand the anguish of losing a parent to incarceration. She was just nine years old when her father was sent to prison. They had always been very close,

Widespread Trauma in a Poverty-Stricken City

Whenever researchers study childhood trauma, poverty is always among the leading causes. Children who live in families that struggle to pay for food, housing, and other basic living expenses have a high risk of enduring traumatic events, often in multiple ways. One city with an extremely high prevalence of poverty—and associated childhood trauma—is Philadelphia, Pennsylvania. Studies have consistently found Philadelphia to have a high prevalence of ACEs, including one study from the fall of 2013 that found 80 percent of the city's children had been exposed to at least one traumatic experience. That can be compared to a national average of 46 percent of children.

Arturo Zinny, who directs the Philadelphia Alliance for Child Trauma Services, says it is "a conservative estimate" that approximately thirty thousand Philadelphia youth have been traumatized and need to be treated for it. "A lot of our kids are living in this constant adversity and having to bounce back from multiple traumatic events," says Zinny. He says all kinds of serious trauma affect Philadelphia children, including community violence; domestic violence; emotional, physical, and sexual abuse; neglect; "and the impact of living in deep poverty."

Quoted in Julia Terruso, "How a North Philly 8-Year-Old Girl, Traumatized by Fire, Found Help," *Philadelphia Inquirer*, April 13, 2018. www.philly.com.

and she loved his goofy sense of humor and the way they joked together. When he took her trick-or-treating on Halloween, for instance, he always dressed as either Yoda or Darth Vader from *Star Wars*. They also had many fun times at Dave & Buster's, a restaurant and video arcade that was their special place. When her dad was suddenly gone, it was as if a hole had been ripped in Young's life. "I was so upset," she says. "I felt abandoned."[12]

> "Whether a child's parent is currently or previously incarcerated, the implications are long-lasting and life-altering."[11]
>
> —Criminal justice advocate Renee Menart

As an African American teen, Young is well aware that people form judgments about others on the basis of race. She was terrified of what kids at school would think of her if they knew about her dad being in prison, so she never told anyone. "I didn't want to tell anybody what I was going through because I thought they would not like me anymore," she says. "I felt like they would stop being friends with me; I thought they would judge me."[13] As time has gone by, she has worked through these issues. Especially therapeutic was writing a book called *The Teen Guide to Living with Incarcerated Parents*, which was published in 2018. Young hopes the book will help other teens who have lost a parent to incarceration.

Unspeakable Trauma

Of all the types of trauma young people experience, one is considered particularly horrific: sexual abuse. It is a topic that makes people cringe, and many often avoid discussing it altogether. But it is important for the public to be aware that tens of thousands of children throughout the United States are victims of sexual abuse each year, and they are deeply scarred by it. According to the Rape, Abuse & Incest National Network (RAINN), there is evidence that among children and youth under age eighteen, an estimated one out of every nine girls and one out of every fifty-three boys were sexually abused by an adult during 2016.

One of these victims was a girl named Jeannette, who says that her father started sexually abusing her when she was very young. "You won't find one picture of me as a child smiling," she says, "not one. The power and pain of living a life of such violence, shame and secrecy was too much for someone so young to carry."[14] Jeannette's father sexually abused her until she was eleven years old, when her mother finally divorced him. Yet even after her nightmare had ended, Jeannette continued to be haunted by guilt and shame. She had no idea how prevalent childhood sexual abuse was, or that many other children had also suffered just as she had. "I thought this only happened in our family," she says. "No one ever talked about it. . . . It was a scary and horrible time in my life."[15]

"No one ever talked about it. . . . It was a scary and horrible time in my life."[15]

—Jeannette, a teen who was sexually abused by her father

As is common among sexual abuse victims, Jeannette turned to self-injury in a futile attempt to feel in control and to numb her emotional pain. "I was not equipped to deal with the strong emotions that started to surface around the abuse," she says. "Self injuring is the single biggest regret of my life. I have had to live with the scars every day. The scars remind me of the pain."[16] As tough as those scars are to look at, however, Jeannette says they remind her of how far she has come.

Scarred by Violence

Of all the sources of childhood trauma that researchers have identified, some of the most violent are also the rarest. This is true of living through a natural or human-made disaster and of exposure to extreme violence, such as a mass shooting at school. In a 2018 *Washington Post* article, reporters John Woodrow Cox and Steven Rich write, "School shootings remain extremely rare, representing a tiny fraction of [America's] gun violence epidemic."[17] Yet as rare as school shootings may be, the statistics about them are still astonishing. During a 2018 investigation by the *Washington Post* reporters, they found that since the 1999 shooting at Columbine High School in Littleton, Colorado, more than 187,000 primary and secondary school students in the United States have experienced a shooting on campus during school hours. For these traumatized young people, the rarity of school shootings means nothing, because they have experienced the horrors firsthand.

Fifteen-year-old Brooke Harrison is one of those students. On February 14, 2018, she was in her fourth-period honors English class at Marjory Stoneman Douglas High School in Parkland, Florida. It was Valentine's Day, so she and her friends were celebrating, giving each other heart-shaped chocolates and teddy bears. "The day was full of love," says Harrison, "which makes the tragedy that occurred even worse."[18] That tragedy was a shooting at her school by a killer wielding an AR-15 semiautomatic rifle. By the time the massacre was over, fourteen students and three staff members were dead, and seventeen others were wounded.

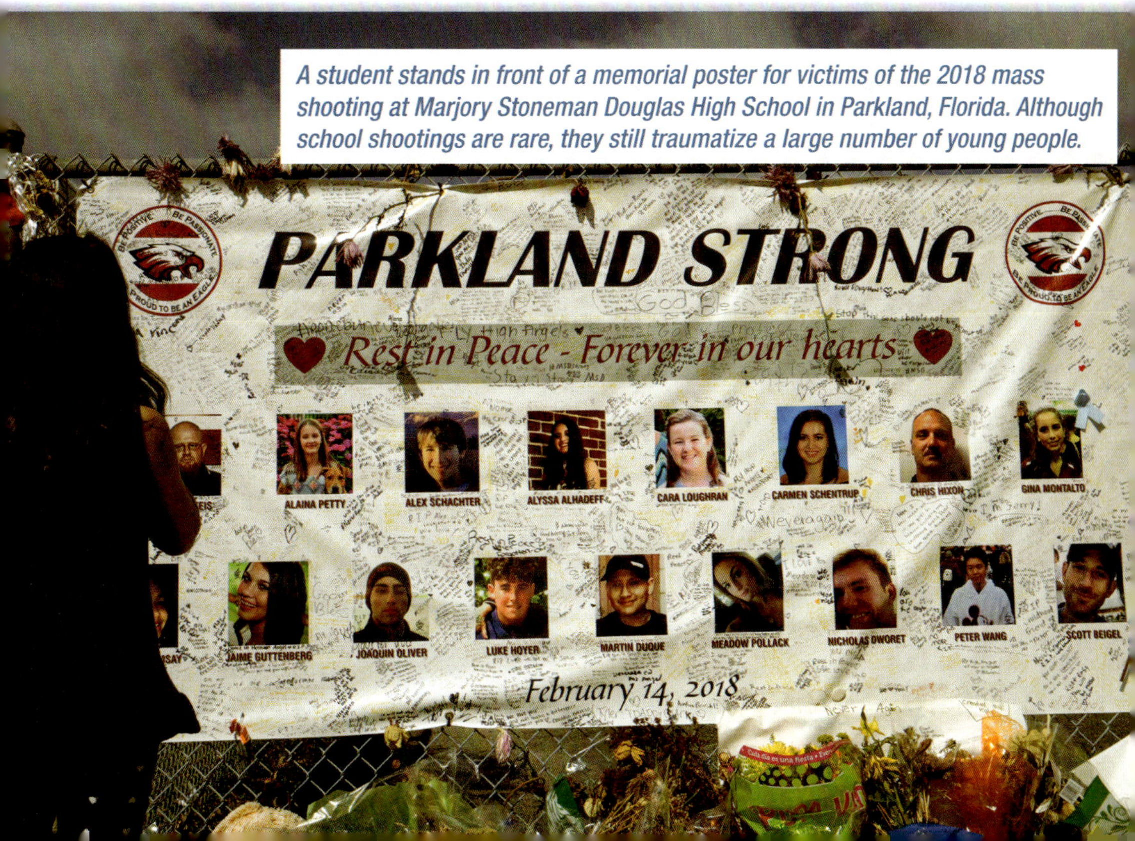

A student stands in front of a memorial poster for victims of the 2018 mass shooting at Marjory Stoneman Douglas High School in Parkland, Florida. Although school shootings are rare, they still traumatize a large number of young people.

> "We were children that came out survivors of war."[19]
>
> —Brooke Harrison, a Parkland, Florida, teenager who survived a shooting at her high school

Harrison will never forget what she saw and heard that day: the deafening sound of gunshots, the terrifying vision of the gunman peering through a window into her classroom, the heartache of being next to one of her best friends who was shot and killed. "Not a single second goes by where I don't think about her and dread the truth that I'm never seeing her again," says Harrison. She goes on to say, "We were children that came out survivors of war."[19]

How Kids Are Affected by School Lockdowns

As uncommon as school shootings may be, the threat of gun violence is very real. Because of that, schools throughout the United States have implemented policies about lockdowns, which could help save lives in the event of an actual shooting. As these measures become increasingly more common, however, they are contributing to trauma among students.

A lockdown is an emergency measure in response to a known or perceived threat in a school or surrounding community. Although schools have different ways of handling them, the typical lockdown protocol involves securing all entrances and exits and prohibiting anyone from entering or leaving; closing and locking all doors to classrooms; moving students to the safest part of a room, away from windows and doors; and covering windows and doors so an intruder or intruders cannot see inside. All classroom instruction stops, and students are told to stay quiet and hidden.

A 2018 *Washington Post* investigation found that during the 2017–2018 school year, more than 4.1 million students experienced at least one lockdown or lockdown drill at their school. This included students in kindergarten and preschool. The lockdowns that were not drills were ordered for various reasons: police manhunts near campuses, bomb threats, or reports of shots fired nearby. According to reporters Cox and Rich, most of the sixty-two hundred lockdowns identified during the *Washington Post*'s investigation stemmed from anonymous warnings of an impending attack that almost always turned out to be a hoax.

School lockdowns have become a controversial issue because young people can be traumatized by them. This is especially true when students are not told that a lockdown is only

Foster Kids in Turmoil

Childhood trauma is extremely common among foster children. According to the National Council for Adoption, more than 430,000 children and teens in the United States are in foster care. This is often because they have been neglected or abused or were living in families in which there was domestic violence. And while the foster care arrangement is designed to keep young people safe, being taken away from their families and familiar surroundings can be extremely traumatic. Not only are children traumatized by what led to the foster care in the first place, says social worker Chrissy Levine, they also suffer from grief over losing all that was familiar to them. "Even when the abuse and neglect is bad," she says, "that's what their normal looks like, so when you take them away from their primary attachment, that to them is the most traumatic thing."

Because of the trauma they have endured, foster children are six times more likely than other children to have behavioral problems. This is not their fault; it has resulted from the lifestyle disruptions and turmoil they have endured. And sometimes when they misbehave, they are simply kids being kids. But they are often judged more harshly than biological children. "Because of the stigma," says Levine, "these kids make a bad decision and the foster parent says, 'I can't handle this; they need to leave my home.'" For foster children, that is a painfully familiar occurrence—and it traumatizes them even more.

Quoted in Jenny Rough, "Childhood Trauma Brings Its Own Health Problems for Foster Families," *Washington Post*, September 1, 2018. www.washingtonpost.com.

a drill. This happened on December 6, 2018, at Lake Brantley High School in Florida. Administrators initiated a "code red" lockdown, announced over the public address system that it was not a drill, and sent teachers a text message that warned of an active shooter on campus. Terrified students hid in classrooms and sobbed hysterically. Some even texted farewell messages to their parents. Later, says journalist Erika Christakis, it was revealed "to the fury of parents, teachers, and students, that in fact this *was* a drill, the most realistic in a series of drills that the students of Lake Brantley, like students across the country, have lately endured."[20]

Although most children are not likely to suffer serious problems from such realistic drills or from lockdowns, trauma experts say that a meaningful percentage will. One who is concerned about this is child psychiatrist and Harvard Medical School professor Steven Schlozman, who refers to the number of lockdowns during the 2017–2018 school year as "staggering." Schlozman says these measures can potentially cause severe trauma for young people:

> We have very good data that children in proximity to frightening circumstances, such as those that trigger school lockdowns, are at risk for lasting symptoms. These include everything from worsening academic and social progression to depression, anxiety, poor sleep, post-traumatic [stress disorder], and substance abuse. Given the potential scope of the problem, we are in dire need of more information. How do we protect children from these issues?[21]

Indeed, school administrators throughout the United States are faced with the complex, daunting challenge of keeping students safe but without traumatizing them in the process.

An Issue of Vital Importance

Schlozman is one of numerous experts who view childhood trauma as a problem that is serious enough to be considered a public health issue. An alarming variety of experiences can cause young people severe distress, from poverty to parental incarceration to physical or sexual abuse to being exposed to violence—the list goes on and on. As time goes by and studies reveal more about this disheartening issue, hopefully children can be better protected from the circumstances that traumatize them.

The Aftermath of Trauma

There are numerous experiences that traumatize children, and among the most painful is the death of a parent. This was true for a New York City boy named Ben who not only lost his father but witnessed him being hit by a car and killed. The accident happened during the summer of 2017 when Ben had just finished first grade. Afterward, his anguish over losing his dad was worsened by the upheaval in his life. His mother became severely depressed and withdrawn, and she stopped working. Without her income the family lost their home, so Ben, his mother, and his two sisters had to move in with relatives who lived in a two-bedroom apartment far from their old neighborhood. Getting to and from school was a two-hour commute, and Ben was late almost every day. When he got home in the evening, his mother was either sleeping or watching television. No one asked how his day went, whether he had homework, or how he was doing. He was exhausted all the time and often fell asleep at night without having dinner. Yet he had trouble sleeping because the apartment was noisy and he had to share a bed with several other children.

It can be devastating for a child to endure such trauma, and it took a heavy toll on Ben. He reacted by lashing out and behaving badly at school. He was disruptive, defying the teacher, knocking books off other students' desks, kicking chairs, and refusing to obey classroom rules. As annoying as this behavior was for Ben's teacher, it was a normal response to the painful traumatic events he had experienced. "Students impacted by trauma struggle to express and control their emotions," says New York City teacher and writer Laura DeInnocentiis. "Some may isolate while others may dominate or bully others. They crave meaning-

Children who are traumatized have a deep need to be understood and accepted, but often end up alone and friendless.

ful interactions, but often misinterpret social cues when trying to build a relationship, which can trigger inappropriate reactions. Consequently, these children often remain alone, friendless, and misunderstood."[22]

Behavior and Learning Challenges

Ben's reaction to what happened in his life is characteristic of children who have experienced trauma. Whether they lose a parent, have been abused, live in poverty, or are affected by some kind of violence, their behavior issues are typical. Trauma can lead to stunted emotional development, poor performance in school, unruly behavior, and innumerable other issues, including emotional and physical illness. "Literally, ACEs can make you sick,"[23] says Martha Davis, senior program officer with philanthropic health organization the Robert Wood Johnson Foundation.

> "Students impacted by trauma struggle to express and control their emotions. . . . Some may isolate while others may dominate or bully others."[22]
>
> —Laura DeInnocentiis, a teacher and writer from New York City

Children in Peril

Children who are separated from their parents can be severely traumatized. This is especially true for younger children; research shows that the younger they are, the more devastating the trauma can be. For that reason, a large group of medical professionals, corporate executives, and business organizations voiced their strong objections to the "zero-tolerance" immigration policy implemented by the administration of President Donald J. Trump in April 2018. The policy, which was intended to deter illegal immigration, required that immigrant children be separated from their parents at the border between the United States and Mexico. Those who objected to the policy emphasized that children would suffer extreme emotional distress by being taken away from their parents. In June 2018 American Medical Association (AMA) chair James L. Madara sent a letter to Trump administration officials, urging them to withdraw the policy. Madara's letter stated:

> Administration's policy will do great harm to children and their parents or caregivers, who felt compelled to make a dangerous and uncertain journey because of safety concerns in their own countries. Families seeking refuge in the U.S. already endure emotional and physical stress, which is only exacerbated when they are separated from one another. It is well known that childhood trauma and adverse childhood experiences created by inhumane treatment often create negative health impacts that can last an individual's entire lifespan. Therefore, the AMA believes strongly that, in the absence of immediate physical or emotional threats to the child's well-being, migrating children should not be separated from their parents or caregivers.

Quoted in American Medical Association, "AMA Urges Administration to Withdraw 'Zero Tolerance' Policy," June 20, 2018. www.ama-assn.org.

According to child and adolescent psychiatrist Nancy Rappaport, traumatized children, especially those who have been neglected or abused, often have problems forming meaningful relationships with teachers. In fact, their trauma has taught them the wisdom of being wary of adults, even those who might seem to be trustworthy. This is a self-protective mechanism that results from being treated badly by people they once trusted and depended on. Also, says Rappaport, traumatized children often develop destructive thinking—the belief that they are bad and that the trauma they endured was somehow their fault. These children often refuse to participate in classroom activities because they are terrified of making a mistake, as she explains: "A mistake that might seem trivial to us becomes magnified if their experience has been that minor mistakes incurred adult anger or punishment."[24]

Clinical psychologist Mona Delahooke speaks of a four-year-old boy named Wyatt who was having severe behavioral issues at his preschool. He suddenly started defying directions and demanding more attention than usual. Nap time was especially challenging, as Delahooke writes: "He would slither on the floor, trying to avoid his cot, in the process disturbing others trying to sleep. Frustrated, his teachers would ask him to stop bothering others, giving him [a] few minutes to comply. When Wyatt didn't comply, a teacher or helper would try physically directing him back to his cot." Upon being directed back to his cot, Wyatt panicked and began kicking anyone who was close by. When someone tried to restrain him, the boy kicked and fought back even harder. Eventually, school officials asked Wyatt's parents to remove him from the preschool. "What his teachers didn't know," says Delahooke, "was that Wyatt's parents were going through a divorce, and he had been listening to them argue violently every night for months."[25]

How Trauma Harms the Brain

When exposed to such a hostile environment, a child can become fearful, anxious, and deeply unhappy. If the trauma continues to happen on a regular basis, it can lead to physical changes to the brain—which in some cases are permanent. "We know

> "We know that long-term stress may alter the brain, even alter (it) irreversibly."[26]
>
> —Jacek Debiec, a neuroscientist and psychiatrist who has treated children and teens who suffer from trauma

that long-term stress may alter the brain, even alter (it) irreversibly,"[26] says Jacek Debiec, a neuroscientist and psychiatrist who has treated children and teens who suffer from trauma.

When babies are born, their brains are still developing. This development continues throughout childhood and adolescence and is not complete until sometime during a person's twenties. Because the brain is still undeveloped during childhood, it is extremely vulnerable to the effects of experiences—both bad and good. That is why trauma presents such a grave risk to young children, especially for babies and toddlers up to age three, when more than 1 million new neural connections are formed every second. Neural connections are links between brain cells known as neurons, of which there are an estimated 100 billion. According to Harvard University's Center on the Developing Child, these neural connections are formed through the interaction of genes and a baby's environment and experiences, especially "serve and return" interactions with their parents and other caregivers. The Center on the Developing Child website explains:

> Serve and return interactions shape brain architecture. When an infant or young child babbles, gestures, or cries, and an adult responds appropriately with eye contact, words, or a hug, neural connections are built and strengthened in the child's brain that support the development of communication and social skills. Much like a lively game of tennis, volleyball, or Ping-Pong, this back-and-forth is both fun and capacity-building. When caregivers are sensitive and responsive to a young child's signals and needs, they provide an environment rich in serve and return experiences.[27]

When a child is subjected to repetitive trauma, by contrast, his or her fight-or-flight response becomes overactive. This leads to what is known as toxic stress, meaning excessive or prolonged activation of stress response systems in the body and brain. Toxic stress can be extremely harmful to a brain that is young and still not fully developed. Brain scans have shown that after exposure to severe, prolonged stress, a section of the brain known as the amygdala, which is important for processing strong emotions such as fear, becomes enlarged and hyperactive—like fear stuck in overdrive. Another part of the brain affected by prolonged stress is the hippocampus, which plays important roles in learning and

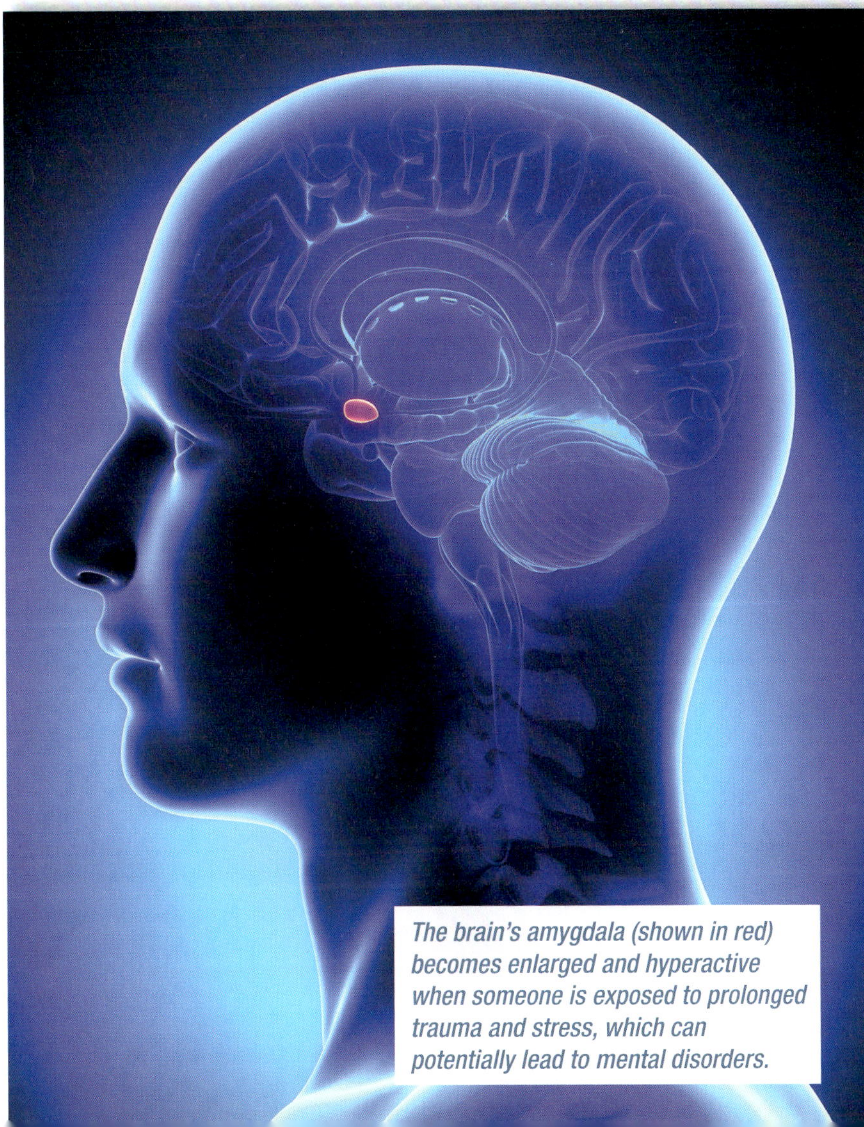

The brain's amygdala (shown in red) becomes enlarged and hyperactive when someone is exposed to prolonged trauma and stress, which can potentially lead to mental disorders.

memory. According to Debiec, brain scans of children who have been traumatized have shown shrinkage in the hippocampus, which means, he says, "that the child . . . may have problems with learning, with staying focused, and with many tasks that require learning and memory, including unlearning previous traumatic experiences."[28]

Research has uncovered another startling fact about childhood trauma and the brain: Young people who are bullied are at risk for mental illness because of bullying's impact on the brain. This was the finding of a study by European researchers who

ADHD or ACEs?

The condition known as attention-deficit/hyperactive disorder (ADHD) occurs most often in children. According to a 2018 publication by the Centers for Disease Control and Prevention (CDC), an estimated 6.1 million children and adolescents living in the United States were diagnosed with ADHD in 2016. As the prevalence of ADHD diagnoses have soared since the 1990s, some mental health professionals question whether these children actually have the disorder or have been mistakenly diagnosed. A typical reason for this skepticism is that the symptoms of ADHD are very similar to behaviors exhibited by children who have been traumatized. Both involve the inability to focus, trouble paying attention, impulsivity, reacting rather than thinking actions through, and hyperactivity.

Pediatrician and noted childhood trauma expert Nadine Burke Harris has had numerous children referred to her for ADHD evaluation by teachers, principals, and counselors. Based on how the children were acting, the referrers assumed they had ADHD. They told her, "This child is having terrible behavior problems. Lots of difficulties with impulse control. Can you put him on Ritalin?" But, says Harris, "when I did a thorough history and physical exam, for most of my patients I could not make the diagnosis of A.D.H.D. The diagnostic criteria for attention-deficit disorder says it can't be caused by anything else. For my kids there was an extremely strong thread: So many were being exposed to very high doses of adversity."

Quoted in David Bornstein, "Opinion: Treating the Lifelong Harm of Childhood Trauma," *New York Times*, January 30, 2018. www.nytimes.com.

analyzed brain scans of nearly seven hundred teens aged fourteen to nineteen from England, Ireland, France, and Germany. The participants completed surveys at ages fourteen, sixteen, and nineteen, to report any experience with bullying. Brain scans were done at ages fourteen and nineteen. Of the participants, thirty-six teens (about 5 percent) were victims of chronic bullying.

The brain scans revealed that at age nineteen—but not at age fourteen—the teens who had been bullied had shrinkage in two key regions of the brain. These regions, known as the caudate and putamen, are involved in regulating motivation, attention, and emotional processing. The changes were detected only in the brains of teens who had been bullied. "We don't know how early in life these brain changes begin," says study author Erin Burke Quinlan, who is with the Center for Population Neuroscience and Precision Medicine at King's College London, in England. "But the earlier bullying is identified, and the sooner it can be dealt with, the better."[29]

Trying to Numb the Pain

Being bullied at a young age has also been linked to substance abuse during adolescence. This was revealed during a study published in the June 2017 issue of *Pediatrics* by researchers from the University of Delaware. The purpose of the study was to determine whether young people who had been bullied eventually abused drugs and/or alcohol or used tobacco products. The researchers analyzed the behavior of 4,297 youth from Birmingham, Alabama; Houston, Texas; and Los Angeles County, California, as the children made their way through school from fifth to tenth grade. The students who were frequently bullied during fifth grade were found to have a high likelihood of developing depression symptoms in the seventh grade. When these same students reached tenth grade, a large percentage started using alcohol, marijuana, and/or tobacco. According to lead study author and social psychologist Valerie Earnshaw, this transition from depression to substance abuse suggests that young people who are

Children who are traumatized have a high risk of abusing drugs and alcohol when they are teens.

bullied "may be self-medicating by using substances to relieve these negative emotions."[30]

Bullying is one of many traumatic experiences that have been linked to teen substance abuse. Research has also shown that children who are abused or are exposed to domestic violence in their families have a much higher likelihood of experimenting with drugs and alcohol than do teens not affected by such trauma. Exploring this was the focus of a 2016 study by researchers from Columbia University, which involved nearly ten thousand adolescents. The study revealed that childhood trauma, especially abuse and domestic violence, vastly increased the chances that teens would try cocaine, marijuana, and other drugs. "Abuse and domestic violence were particularly harmful to children, increasing the chances of all types of drug use in the adolescent years,"[31] says study coauthor Hannah Carliner. She adds, though, that other types of trauma, such as car accidents, natural disasters, and major childhood illness, also increased the chances that teens would use illicit drugs.

A young man named Brad, whose childhood was a nightmare of abuse and neglect, started drinking heavily while he was in high school. That eventually led to abusing drugs, as he explains: "I didn't start drinking until late in high school, but when I did it opened up the floodgates to all kinds of substance use. Anything that would make me feel good, I would do. MDMA, cocaine, Oxy—put something in front of me that could make me escape and I would snort it, swallow it, and, eventually, inject it." At the time, Brad did not connect his drug use with being traumatized by abuse as a child; it did not even occur to him. "I wasn't calling my dealer thinking, 'I'm doing this because my parents abused me,'" he says. Eventually, his friends tapered off on their alcohol and drug use, but Brad kept going. "For me, it didn't stop," he says. "It was the only way to feel the way I wanted to feel. And it took me a long time to connect that to what happened when I was a kid."[32] Once he was able to make that connection, his life began to change for the better.

> "I didn't start drinking until late in high school, but when I did it opened up the floodgates to all kinds of substance use."[32]
>
> —A young man named Brad who was abused and neglected as a child

The Unimaginable Pain of Sexual Abuse

Like Brad, a young woman named Laura developed a substance abuse problem as a result of childhood trauma. For her, the substance was alcohol, and the trauma she tried to drink away was sexual abuse. When Laura thinks back on her childhood, she envisions a sharp dividing line—one that separates the before from the after. "I would remember my life before the sexual abuse and it felt like a dream I wanted to return to," she says. "I remember what it was like to feel safe, to not feel angry, sad, and alone, and

I want[ed] to return to that place. When I got older, I discovered that alcohol could only temporarily give me refuge." Laura was only seven years old when the sexual abuse started, and she turned to alcohol as a young teenager. She says that for a little while, the alcohol numbed her sadness and anger and gave her the solace she was so desperately seeking. "Drinking made me forget," she says. "It made me feel normal. . . . For a little bit, I could be free."[33] But as soon as the effects of the alcohol wore off, Laura once again was faced with the horrors she had to endure as a child. And the vicious cycle continued.

Sexual abuse victims like Laura are four times more likely than nonvictims to become substance abusers, according to RAINN. Children who have been sexually abused are also about four times more likely to develop post-traumatic stress disorder and three times more likely to develop major depression.

For Danielle, the trauma from being sexually abused as a little girl changed her into a completely different person. Before the abuse began, she was outgoing, happy, and trusting. Afterward, she became withdrawn and found it hard to trust adults. "If someone violates your trust in that way, if you witness that kind of cruelty, of course it is natural to become sad, to become suspicious, and to retreat within yourself," says Danielle. "It is a survival mechanism."[34]

> "I was always keyed up and ready to explode in some way. But my sadness, my anger, my inability to relax were assumed to be the normal experiences of an overemotional teenage girl."[35]
>
> —Danielle, a young woman who was sexually abused as a child

As the sexual abuse continued, Danielle changed in other ways. She began having trouble concentrating, and she suffered from memory problems. By the time she entered high school, the abuse had stopped—but the trauma continued to haunt her. Her grades suffered, and learning was difficult even though she was naturally intelligent. Even more distressing were the significant changes in her behavior. She suffered from depression and anxiety, and she often felt aggressive and out of control. "I was always keyed up and ready to explode in some way," says Danielle. "But my sadness, my anger, my inability to relax were assumed to be the normal experiences of an overemotional teenage girl. In fact, I assumed it myself. It becomes easy to hide yourself inside a cliché."[35] When her teenage years were behind her and she did not feel any better, Danielle realized that her problem was not teenage hormones—it was the sexual abuse from her childhood that had traumatized her.

No Way Out

Severe trauma, whether it is caused by sexual abuse, physical abuse, neglect, or other painful experiences, can be unbearable for those who are plagued by it. Although many people who were traumatized as children are successfully treated, some are not able to overcome their deep emotional pain and tragically decide to end their lives. Researchers who study suicide have found that teens and young adults who were traumatized as children have a significantly higher risk of suicidal thinking and attempted suicide than those who never suffered from childhood trauma.

This was revealed during a 2018 study by researchers from the University of Leeds in the United Kingdom. One hundred sixty people participated in the study and were divided into three groups: those who had attempted suicide, those who had had thoughts of suicide but had not attempted it, and those who had neither thought about nor attempted suicide. The researchers found that of the people who had attempted suicide, nearly 80 percent had experienced at least one type of trauma as children. Of those who had only thought about suicide but never attempted it, 40 percent had a history of childhood trauma. And of participants who had never given any thought to suicide, only 20 percent had experienced trauma as children.

One young man who took his life after being haunted by childhood trauma was nineteen-year-old Nathan Smith. He was adopted at age thirteen by a loving family who provided him with a happy home and stable environment. But before that, he had spent many tumultuous years being shuffled from one foster home or group home to another. After he committed suicide in August 2018, Nate's adoptive mother, Amy Smith, wrote an obituary for him, saying that years of trauma and instability proved impossible for him to overcome. She explained that as hard as he tried, and as hard as she and others tried to help him, Nate "could not escape the trauma he experienced. A young man with a wide, easy smile that masked the pain he carried into every space. He spent much of his time anxious and depressed, angry and exhausted."[36] Because of the childhood trauma that he could not forget, said Amy, Nate never stopped being convinced that he was unworthy of kindness, peace, joy, or love. Eventually, the pain became more than he was able to bear.

Lasting Scars

Childhood trauma is a horrible, heartbreaking thing. "Trauma experienced in childhood," says psychiatrist David Sack, "has a special ability to wound."[37] It can alter brain structure and interfere with a child's normal brain development, which in turn affects memory and the ability to learn. Being traumatized can lead to behavioral problems, depression, and other mental illnesses and often results in people turning to drugs or alcohol in a desperate attempt to feel better. In the most tragic cases, someone with a history of trauma may become convinced that the misery will never end and ultimately decide that death would be better than the excruciating pain of living. That is not a common fate among childhood trauma victims—but even one life tragically cut short is one too many.

Harm That Can Last a Lifetime

There is an old belief that children have some innate ability to bounce back from the problems and disappointments they encounter. This ability is known as resilience, and although many children do possess it, they are not born with it. They become stronger and more resilient over time by overcoming obstacles and learning from their mistakes and frustrations. But for those who are physically or sexually abused, are neglected, or endure other types of trauma, bouncing back may be impossible. "People used to think that children were resilient by virtue of being young," says child and adolescent psychiatrist Victor G. Carrion. "The reality cannot be further from the truth. The younger you are the more vulnerable you are to the effects of trauma."[38]

> "The younger you are the more vulnerable you are to the effects of trauma."[38]
>
> —Child and adolescent psychologist Victor G. Carrion

Today health care professionals widely agree that trauma experienced during childhood can be devastating over the long term. It can lead to mental disorders and physical illnesses during adolescence, as well as throughout adulthood. Dave Brethauer, a wellness coach from Chicago, Illinois, is convinced that his serious emotional and medical issues are rooted in the abuse he suffered as a child. "From the time I was five till 14 I had an abusive stepdad in my life,"[39] he says. Now in his sixties, Brethauer spent decades trying to blot out his painful past with destructive practices and habits. He drank too much and became addicted to alcohol. He developed an addiction to food, sex, and even exercise. At least once he contemplated suicide and spent

It was long believed that children could bounce back from being traumatized, but that has been debunked. In reality, the younger children are when experiencing trauma, the more vulnerable they are to its harmful effects.

time in the locked ward of a psychiatric hospital. Then when he was fifty, Brethauer was diagnosed with type 2 diabetes, which can increase the risk of kidney damage, stroke, and heart disease. The diagnosis was a shock for Brethauer, because it showed him how much damage his traumatic childhood had caused.

Groundbreaking Research

The connection between childhood trauma and diseases of the mind and body is well understood today, but scientists first became aware of it only in the mid-1990s. A major public health study confirmed that traumatic experiences in childhood were disturbingly common. In addition, the study showed a clear association between such experiences and an astounding array of disorders and diseases. Public health researcher Shanta R. Dube, who was involved in the study, says it "provided insight into the lifelong health consequences of adverse childhood experiences (ACEs). It was the beginning of our understanding that these experiences can have negative effects on childhood development, leading to physical and mental health problems throughout life."[40]

The landmark ACE study grew out of a discovery by Vincent Felitti, a San Diego, California, physician. Felitti specialized in preventive medicine, and during the 1980s he supervised a weight loss program in San Diego. The program was for severely obese individuals, people who were from 100 pounds (45.4 kg) to 600 pounds (272.2 kg) overweight. Felitti became mystified when a high number of these participants dropped out of the program once they started losing weight. It made no sense to him, so he began interviewing patients. After speaking with 286 of them, he learned that nearly all had been sexually abused as children. One of the patients, Ella Herman, told Felitti in a letter, "I suffered for years. The pain became so great I was thinking of jumping off the San Diego Bay Bridge."[41]

For Herman and others who dropped out of Felitti's program, eating was a source of comfort that soothed their fears, depression, and anxiety, much like drinking alcohol or taking drugs. When they cut back on eating—which was necessary to lose weight—their source of comfort was gone, and they once again became anxious, depressed, and fearful.

What Felitti had discovered caught the attention of Robert F. Anda, a physician with the CDC. Both doctors suspected that childhood trauma was associated not only with obesity but also with many other health issues. So they initiated a major research project called the CDC–Kaiser Permanente Adverse Childhood Experiences Study. More than seventeen thousand patients who visited the Kaiser Permanente health maintenance organization in San Diego completed questionnaires about their health behaviors, including answering questions about their experiences with childhood trauma. Roughly one-third of them reported having no childhood trauma in their past, while the remainder had experienced from one to eight ACEs.

The study produced a wealth of information about childhood trauma and its effects. It showed, for instance, a strong association between childhood trauma and substance abuse among teens, as well as higher numbers of suicide attempts among teens who had been traumatized as children. But the findings went beyond health issues during adolescence and also revealed a great deal about problems that persisted into adulthood. ACEs were linked to a number of health issues, including heart disease, liver disease, cancer, stroke, chronic obstructive pulmonary disease, intravenous drug use, depression, and other behavioral illnesses. The study also yielded some truly shocking correlations. The researchers found that compared with people who had no ACEs in their history, those with four or more were 700 percent more likely to become alcoholics—and 1,200 percent more likely to attempt suicide.

Shortened Life Span

The landmark ACE study proved invaluable to researchers and paved the way for numerous other studies. One published in October 2009, for example, explored whether childhood trauma was linked to an increased risk of premature death. In the decade after publication of the ACE study, researchers kept records of which of the 17,337 participants had died. They found that 1,539 of the participants had passed away during the ten-year period. Those who reported extremely high levels of childhood trauma (six or more ACEs) lived an average of sixty years, whereas those with fewer ACEs lived nearly eighty years—a loss of twenty years from their lifespan that was closely linked to the severe trauma they experienced during childhood.

The researchers theorized that the participants who died earlier were those whose traumatic childhoods had led to risky health habits and negative lifestyle choices. Anda, who was also involved in the 2009 study, explains, "They tend to take on the risk factors that lead to poor health. They smoke more, they are more likely to abuse alcohol, use illicit drugs . . . or to be overweight or to

Still Haunted by the Past

Samantha Haviland is a counselor with the Denver Public Schools system in Colorado. She has spent nearly her entire career working with traumatized kids but kept her own trauma to herself. In April 1999, when Haviland was sixteen and a junior at Columbine High School in Littleton, Colorado, she was in the cafeteria laughing and talking with friends. Suddenly two girls burst in, screaming that someone had a gun and was shooting. Haviland and her friends hid in the back of an auditorium, cringing at the sound of gunfire. She narrowly avoided being shot by choosing not to run down a particular corridor—one where the two gunmen were slaughtering anyone they encountered.

Haviland escaped death that day, but as traumatized as she was, she never sought counseling. She believed she did not deserve it because so many of her classmates had been killed or wounded. But an incident in 2008 convinced her that, even nine years later, she needed help. Her school held a drill, and as she crouched on the floor of a room with the lights off and the door locked, she had a panic attack. *Washington Post* reporters John Woodrow Cox and Steven Rich write, "She heard footsteps. Then, beneath the door, she saw the shadow of an administrator who was checking the locks. Her chest began to throb, and her body began to quake and, suddenly, Haviland knew she wouldn't be okay." Finally, she accepted that the only way she would overcome the trauma was to seek professional help.

John Woodrow Cox and Steven Rich, "Scarred by School Shootings," *Washington Post*, March 25, 2018. www.washingtonpost.com.

be physically inactive." Also, says Anda, "They're twice as likely to die by 65 years than people who had none of those adverse childhood experiences."[42]

Binge Eating and Obesity

As research has consistently shown, one health problem that is closely associated with childhood trauma is obesity. Felitti observed this decades ago among participants at his obesity clinic, and research since that time has further supported the theory. "If

> "If you were abused or not properly cared for as a child, and you now struggle with overeating, you are not alone."[43]
>
> —Psychologist Elizabeth Hartney

you were abused or not properly cared for as a child, and you now struggle with overeating, you are not alone," says psychologist Elizabeth Hartney. She adds that many obese people suffer from binge eating disorder. This is a type of eating disorder that shares many characteristics with addictive behaviors, including the lack of control and continued overeating despite negative consequences. "We know there is a strong association between childhood abuse and binge eating disorders," says Hartney, "as well as between childhood abuse and other eating disorders, addictions, and mental health problems."[43]

Exploring the link between childhood trauma and addictive eating in adulthood was the focus of a 2013 study that involved more than fifty-seven thousand women. The women were all registered nurses who had participated in the Nurses' Health Study. The research revealed that addictive eating behaviors were relatively common among the women. About 8 percent of participants met the diagnostic criteria for food addiction, which is defined as three or more addiction-like eating behaviors that are severe enough to cause significant distress or loss of function. Women who had been physically or sexually abused as children were almost twice as likely to have a food addiction during middle age compared with women who did not have a history of childhood abuse.

Another finding was that the likelihood of food addiction was higher in women who had experienced both physical and sexual abuse during childhood. And women with a food addiction were generally heavier than women without a food addiction. In an interview after the study was released, lead author Susan A. Mason said, "We are becoming more and more aware of the long-term health consequences associated with childhood abuse. But we need a better understanding of the psychological reasons why some women who are victims of this abuse appear to overeat as a coping strategy."[44]

Trinity Wallace-Ellis was about eight years old when she began to associate food with comfort and consolation. Her mother had abandoned the family two years before, and her father, a heroin addict, was violent and abusive and sometimes beat Trinity and her younger sisters. Afterward, he regretted his actions and attempted to show his remorse by filling the refrigerator with cakes and pies. "From that point, I think, is when I equated food with comfort and food as a way of making things right," she says. Now in her forties, Wallace-Ellis says that throughout her entire life she has battled her weight. At times she weighed more than 400 pounds (181.4 kg). "There was nothing else that could soothe me,"[45] she says of her reliance on food. Although she has now learned healthier methods of coping, her years-long battle with obesity took its toll. She suffers from both high blood pressure and diabetes.

Research has shown a strong link between childhood trauma and binge eating and obesity during the adult years.

Trauma and Mental Illness

Whether childhood trauma should be considered an urgent public health issue is often debated. But as research continues to grow, and more links between trauma and health problems become clear, support for such a designation grows as well. This was true after publication of a study in November 2018 that linked mental illness to early childhood trauma. In an editorial that accompanied the study, psychologist Marc Gelkopf writes, "The chance of developing psychotic features in adulthood after child abuse surpasses, by far, any other causally implied biological factor cited in the literature regarding the development of schizophrenia in adulthood."[46]

Desperate Attempt to Escape

One of the health issues that has been associated with childhood trauma is alcohol abuse. Many people who are haunted by traumatic experiences from the past turn to heavy drinking in an attempt to blot out painful memories. This was true of Russ Taff, who grew up in a small California farming community with abusive parents and a father known for drunken rages. The elder Taft was a Pentecostal preacher who denounced alcohol consumption in fiery sermons—while at the same time going on regular drinking binges. Taff remembers him screaming at his mother, calling her terrible names, and threatening to shoot her. Taff and his younger brother would crawl under their bunk bed and cower there, praying their father would not come into their room and unleash his rage on them. When Taff told a friend about his parents' arguments, his mother beat him severely. She also hit him in the mouth if he dared to criticize his father, no matter how abusive he was to his family.

When Taff was in his twenties, he launched a music career and also started drinking heavily. For years he continued to abuse alcohol, and it nearly ruined his life. Finally he sought treatment, which involved facing the years of abuse and pain he had suffered as a child. Today he is a Grammy Award–winning Christian singer who feels that he is finally at peace with his traumatic childhood.

The researchers analyzed data collected while the participants were children and whatever happened to them, good or bad, was fresh in their minds. They continued analyzing data for years afterward. All in all, this analysis period lasted for twenty-two years. Of the 1,420 participants, 31 percent had been exposed to one traumatic event by age sixteen, 22.5 percent were exposed to two ACEs, and 14.8 percent were exposed to three or more ACEs. The most common type of trauma reported by participants was witnessing a traumatic event. Others included unintentional life-threatening injuries, learning about a traumatic incident that affected a loved one, physical abuse, and sexual abuse.

> "Our study suggested that childhood trauma casts a long and wide-ranging shadow, showing associations with elevated risk for adult psychiatric status."[47]
>
> —The authors of a 2018 study on childhood trauma

After adjusting for other factors that cause adversity, such as low income and family hardships, the researchers found clear connections between childhood trauma and mental health disorders. These included anxiety disorders, depression, ADHD, oppositional defiant disorder, conduct disorder, and substance abuse. In addition, participants who had experienced trauma as children were more likely to have physical health problems, struggle financially, participate in risky behaviors, and be involved in dysfunctional, often violent, relationships. And as other research has clearly shown, the participants most at risk for health problems of all types were those with multiple childhood traumas. The study authors write, "Our study suggested that childhood trauma casts a long and wide-ranging shadow, showing associations with elevated risk for adult psychiatric status." They go on to offer cautionary words: "It is a myth to believe that childhood trauma is a rare experience that only affects few. . . . Rather, childhood trauma exposure is a normative experience, statistically speaking, that affects the majority of children at some point and subsequently has the potential to influence many aspects of functioning."[47]

Childhood Trauma and Chronic Pain

Innumerable health issues have been associated with childhood trauma, and studies continue to find new associations—such as chronic pain. In 2018 researchers from Pennsylvania State University found a link between trauma experienced by children and chronic pain they suffer as adults. This was an important finding because the CDC reports that an estimated 50 million Americans suffer from chronic pain. "Pain is the number one reason people seek health care in the United States,"[48] says Jennifer Graham-Engeland, one of the researchers.

In 2018 she and her colleagues conducted the study, which involved a diverse group of 265 adults living in the Bronx borough of New York City. All of the participants reported experiencing at least one kind of trauma during their childhood, and some had experienced as many as seven. The types of ACEs they reported varied, with the most common (affecting 44 percent of participants) being a traumatic event that left them frightened for years. The second most common ACE was parental divorce (31 percent of participants), followed by a major illness or accident that required hospitalization (24 percent), parental substance abuse (24 percent), sexual abuse (23 percent), parental unemployment (21 percent), a child's removal from the home (10 percent), and physical abuse (10 percent). Participants were also asked about their current mood, typical sleep patterns, level of optimism, how in control of their lives they felt, and whether they experienced pain.

The study found a strong association between trauma experienced during childhood or adolescence and greater physical pain during adulthood. The researchers learned, however, that participants who felt more optimistic and in control of their lives seemed to better manage their pain, as though they refused to let it control their lives. According to Graham-Engeland, the study builds on a body of research that has shown a link between childhood trauma and pain, and it also shows that resilience is possible—but not necessarily for everyone. She explains, "Some people can be relatively resilient to adverse effects in the longer term, while others have a harder time."[49]

Generation to Generation

With each new ACE study, researchers gain valuable insight into the causes of trauma during childhood and its effects on people's physical and mental health. Some research has focused on how trauma may be passed from one generation to another. "We frequently call this a two-generation or three-generation problem," says Angelo Giardino, who is a professor of pediatrics at Baylor College of Medicine in Houston. "Because not only is the kid exposed to it, it's likely that the adult in their life has experienced

Childhood trauma may be hereditary. Research has shown that children of parents who were traumatized in childhood have an elevated risk of developing ADHD and other mental health problems.

adversity. When you do an intervention, you have to treat everyone—the kids, the parents, and even the grandparents."[50]

In June 2018 researchers from the University of California, Los Angeles, School of Medicine announced the results of a study focused on exploring any possible links between parents who had experienced childhood trauma and behavioral problems in their children. Researchers used data from an earlier survey with information on four generations of American families. Included was whether parents were abused, neglected, or exposed to other types of mistreatment or family dysfunction while growing up, as well as information on any behavioral problems shown in their children. By exploring this data, the researchers found strong associations between the parents' childhood trauma and their children's behavioral health issues. The researchers also discovered that the children of parents who had four or more ACEs had a significantly higher risk of having ADHD and were four times more likely to have mental health problems. "Previous research has looked at childhood trauma as a risk factor for later physical and mental health problems in adulthood," says pediatrician Adam Schickedanz, the study's lead author, "but this is the first research to show that the long-term behavioral health harms of childhood adversity extend across generations from parent to child."[51]

> "This is the first research to show that the long-term behavioral health harms of childhood adversity extend across generations from parent to child."[51]
>
> —Pediatrician Adam Schickedanz

Another finding was that traumatic experiences during a mother's childhood had a stronger negative effect on her children's behavioral health than the father's experiences. Also, parents who lived through traumatic childhoods were more likely to report higher levels of aggravation over parenting and to experience mental health problems than were parents not subjected to trauma as children. But according to the data, these factors accounted for only a small percentage of children's elevated behavioral health risks. The researchers emphasize that further study is needed to examine other possible reasons for the link between parents' ACEs and their children's behavioral health.

Growing Knowledge

In the years since the groundbreaking first ACE study, researchers have aggressively pursued research on childhood trauma and its effects on the lives of people young and old. Since the first major ACE study in the 1990s, an immense amount of knowledge has been gained through research. It is now known, for instance, that childhood trauma is at the root of an alarming range of mental and physical illnesses. Trauma has also been connected to alcoholism, drug addiction, obesity, heightened suicide risk, and even chronic pain. In just over two decades, all that knowledge and more has been gained about childhood trauma and its adverse effects on people who have experienced it. Kathryn Magruder, a disease specialist and professor of psychiatry at the Medical University of South Carolina, believes this research is incredibly convincing: "I think it should put to rest any kind of speculation about early childhood trauma and later life difficulties."[52]

CHAPTER FOUR

The Dire Need for Solutions

The growing awareness of childhood trauma and the immense harm it can cause has led to an urgent call for action. Pediatrician Nadine Burke Harris, one of the nation's leading experts on the issue, is one of the most vocal advocates for solutions to the problem. "This is treatable," she says. "This is beatable. The single most important thing that we need today is the courage to look this problem in the face and say, 'this is real, and this is all of us.'"[53] Harris and other experts emphasize the importance of understanding that children who have been traumatized cannot recover emotionally or physically if the cause of their problems—the trauma they experienced—is not addressed. It is at the root of everything, including their health, their behavior, and their well-being.

Essential Screening

Childhood trauma specialists emphasize that along with the medical care children receive, they should be screened for ACEs. If health care providers find or suspect that a child is a victim of trauma, they can work with the family to address any immediate threats and reduce the likelihood of future threats. Providers can also make referrals to appropriate services, such as counselors, social workers, or family therapy groups, that can help the traumatized child and his or her family. One professional group that strongly recommends trauma screening is the American Academy of Pediatrics (AAP). The academy has called for pediatricians to screen their young patients for any circumstances that could potentially lead to trauma. In addition, the AAP provides a number of tools that pediatricians can use to conduct trauma screening.

Yet despite the AAP's stance and the high prevalence of trauma among children, trauma screening is not a routine part of pediatric primary care. Experts insist that this needs to change. "Studies show that when kids received early high quality intervention, their brain scans ended up looking more like those of children who had never been maltreated than children who had been maltreated," says Harris. "Ultimately, every pediatrician in America needs to be screening for ACEs."[54]

Medical professionals throughout the United States have started to evaluate the value of ACE screening, and many are developing tools for it. These often vary according to the individual facility. At Harvard University and the University of California, San Francisco, for instance, researchers are working on screening tools that can detect the biological markers of toxic stress in children. The intent is to help detect toxic stress earlier, before it can damage a child's brain. "There's no one accepted way to measure the effect of excessive stress activation," says Al Race, deputy director of Harvard University's Center on the Developing Child. Just as with adults, "every child reacts to stress differently."[55]

> "Every child reacts to stress differently."[55]
>
> —Al Race, deputy director of Harvard University's Center on the Developing Child

At community clinics in Marin County, California, children have been screened for ACEs since April 2018. Parents are asked to complete ACE surveys when they take their babies for well-child visits at nine months and thirty months. In addition to babies, pediatric patients new to the clinic are screened up to age twelve years. If the screening tool shows that the baby or child has had more than one or two ACEs, the clinic offers services such as parenting and other support groups, classes in stress management, and individual therapy.

In order to uncover instances of childhood trauma at an early stage, pediatricians are urged to screen children for signs of trauma as a regular part of their medical care.

Trauma screening can also benefit adults because so many diseases and disorders are linked to childhood trauma. In September 2018 family medicine residents at Kaiser Permanente in San Jose, California, began screening adult patients for ACEs. As part of a pilot program, patients complete a short survey about their childhood and any possible trauma. If patients select two or more categories, doctors discuss the possibility of support services for them. Doctors also educate their patients on what has been discovered about ACEs. Physician Kathryn Ridout, who leads the program, explains, "We are sharing that we know ACE exposure can increase your risk for a number of health outcomes by making you more sensitive to stress and that resilience can help modify this risk. We then provide resources available to help build resilience."[56]

Invaluable Therapy

People of all ages who have been traumatized often benefit a great deal from psychotherapy. There are dozens of different kinds, and what works best depends on the patient's unique needs. One type that is often used with trauma patients of all ages is cognitive behavioral therapy (CBT). This psychotherapeutic technique is designed to change distorted, negative thinking patterns that are at the root of people's difficulties, thus helping them change the way they feel. "CBT is based on a model or theory that it's not events themselves that upset us, but the meanings we give them," says psychologist Ben Martin. "If our thoughts are too negative, it can block us seeing things or doing things that don't fit—that disconfirm—what we believe is true. In other words, we continue to hold on to the same old thoughts and fail to learn anything new."[57]

One reason CBT is valuable for trauma survivors is that it involves facing their traumatic experiences head-on—which can be agonizing but is necessary in order to heal. New York psychotherapist Pamela Garber says the only way someone can heal after being subjected to childhood trauma is to remember and understand what happened, as horrid as it may be. She often uses a combination approach, with CBT and psychodynamic therapy, which explores the unconscious mind. "Through CBT, I identify the patient's beliefs about his circumstances and help him recognise how they influence his feelings," she says. "With psychodynamic therapy, I delve into the patient's past, uncovering themes—for instance, a controlling parent or an abusive sibling—that play out in the present day." The next step, says Garber, is to help the patient separate which part of his or her thinking is rational and which part is irrational. "By throwing the irrational aspects out on the table," she says, "clients often discover a gateway to detailed recollection of past experiences that still feel unresolved."[58]

Garber acknowledges that it can be excruciatingly difficult for patients to recall painful, even terrible, events in their lives. And this practice is often a matter of debate among mental health professionals, since recalling traumatic events may cause even more trauma. But, says Garber, "after 17 years of working with survivors of family-of-origin abuse, my bias is that when the events are early and deep, it is almost always vital to recall them, otherwise all work will eventually be sorted back into the long-standing scars."[59]

A Nontraditional Approach

As valuable as traditional therapy can be for many patients, it does not work for some trauma sufferers, who need a different approach. Hospitals and treatment facilities employ a wide variety of therapies in their treatment plans for traumatized patients. At KVC Hospitals in Kansas City, Kansas, for instance, therapists use animal-assisted therapy, art therapy, dance therapy, music therapy, horticulture therapy, and virtual reality, among other types of therapy. Stephen, a teenage boy who had experienced severe trauma as a child, benefited from virtual reality therapy. Because of the trauma in his past, he struggled to control his emotions and was often physically aggressive toward others. According to his therapist, Alicia Armstrong, Stephen had been hospitalized in psychiatric facilities and had spent time at a residential treatment center, and had never felt that therapy helped him. Although he had seen therapists for several years at various mental health facilities, he said it was hard for him to connect with them. But once he tried virtual reality therapy, his progress was truly amazing, as Armstrong explains: "Now, this young boy who had never left the state of Kansas was suddenly able to go anywhere in the world."[60]

Stephen told Armstrong that he had always dreamed of visiting Africa, and virtual reality made him feel as if he were actually there. "During his 'trip' to Africa, he enjoyed walking alongside cheetahs and lions,"[61] she says. As he continued to use virtual reality and grew to trust his therapist, Stephen found the courage to open up about what had happened to him when he was a child. Using Google Earth VR, he took Armstrong to his childhood home and was able to talk about the trauma he had endured there.

Helping a Little Girl Heal

In November 2017 eight-year-old Dakota Johnson had a terrifying experience. While staying with her father at his apartment in Philadelphia, Pennsylvania, she was awakened in the middle of the night to the sounds of screams and the shrieking of an alarm—the apartment was on fire. Dakota and her father tried to get out the front door, but the thick smoke drove them back inside. So he opened the kitchen window, three stories up, and carefully lowered Dakota to the second floor roof. A police officer pulled her to safety, and her father was also rescued.

The incident was horribly traumatic for Dakota. Afterward she cringed anytime she heard sirens, had nightmares, and often cried in the night. She also had frequent stomachaches while at school. Her mom took her to a therapy program that specializes in trauma, and Dakota began seeing a therapist. He worked with her to help her overcome her fears, teaching her deep breathing and relaxation exercises. "Sometimes when I'm scared at night I think there's about to be a fire, but there isn't," says Dakota. Whenever she gets frightened, she remembers what she has learned about breathing. "I have to blow my stomach up and then breathe out of my mouth slowly," she says. The therapy and exercises have helped Dakota heal from her trauma experience. She hopes that in a few years, the fire will be nothing more than a distant memory. "I'll still be a little scared maybe," she says, "but I probably won't be that scared."

Quoted in Jen Kinney, "As Awareness of Childhood Trauma Rises, New Free Therapy Program Launches for Philly Students," WhyY, April 30, 2018. https://whyy.org.

Stephen continued to make progress and began talking to Armstrong about his future. She helped him explore university campuses in virtual reality, and KVC staff took him to tour some so he could see them in real life. He then started talking about becoming a veterinarian so he could help animals, and he also expressed an interest in being a helpful member of society. The boy who initially told Armstrong he felt hopeless, she writes, "started to see new possibilities for his life that he used to think were completely out of his reach. . . . He had a future—and it was a bright one."[62]

Focusing on At-Risk Kids

Like Stephen, millions of children are haunted by trauma because of experiences in their home environments. Whether the problem is severe poverty, neglect, abuse, a combination of those, or other adversities, youngsters are left traumatized. Typically, when parents are unable to provide a safe home environment and/or adequate care, children are removed from the home and placed in foster care. Although it may be the only available option to keep children safe, foster care presents many challenges of its own. Separating children from their caregivers and moving them to unfamiliar surroundings can compound the trauma they have already experienced. Moreover, research has shown that children in the foster care system change homes up to twice a year, and they are twice as likely as kids not in foster care to drop out of high school.

When parents are abusive, their children can be placed in foster care. Although this is done for the children's safety, they can suffer additional trauma from the separation.

One city where this is a particularly serious problem is Washington, DC, where an extraordinarily high number of children have been temporarily removed from their homes and/or placed in foster care at some point during their lives. Upon learning these bleak statistics, economist and educator Emily Bloomfield wanted to do something about the problem. After a long process of planning, gathering supporters, and seeking private and public funding, Bloomfield founded Monument Academy, which provides a therapeutic environment for at-risk children. Monument is a public charter school, different from most charter schools because it provides a home for young people as well as schooling. About 130 children in fifth through eighth grade had participated in the academy's program as of 2019.

During the week, academy students live in single-sex apartments in groups of ten, with house parents who provide them with a warm, structured, and nurturing environment. The children learn manners and social norms, as well as respect for themselves and for each other. By showing progress in these areas, they can earn core values points, as one young resident explains about living with her house parents: "We earn [points] by being kind to one another, being respectful to their daughter, the dogs, the house, and doing what we're supposed to do."[63] On the weekends all students go home. Depending on their individual circumstances, this could be to foster families, parents, or other caregivers.

Bloomfield and other supporters of Monument Academy believe it could be a model for other communities to follow. Such facilities are virtually nonexistent, and there is a pressing need nationwide to help traumatized children. "There aren't many schools that work with this population of students," says Denise Miles, who is Monument's head of school and has been there since its 2015 opening. She goes on to say:

> We have the opportunity to really influence all aspects of a student's life. When I was a high school principal, I often said if I could just rent the house across the street and give them a place that's stable and quiet, where they can do

homework and not have to worry about taking care of siblings or what's going on in the neighborhood or anything else, then we could really move them further faster. Here we can be working on life skills with them, and they're getting counseling, and house parents are doing academic support in the evening. They're learning 24 hours a day.[64]

Legislative Efforts

Because of the high prevalence and seriousness of childhood trauma throughout the United States, many trauma experts have called for government intervention. Officials from some state governments have also expressed interest in legislative measures, especially after reports of nationwide ACE prevalence were released. The National Conference of State Legislatures (NCSL) writes, "Some state policymakers are interested in preventing such [adverse childhood] experiences, mitigating their effects, and reducing the associated costs to state health care, education, child welfare and correctional systems." Policies that are being introduced by states, says the NCSL, "include strategies to build resilience in children and families, help parents reduce stress, and increase screening and treatment for ACE."[65]

> "We have the opportunity to really influence all aspects of a student's life."[64]
>
> —Denise Miles, head of school at Monument Academy in Washington, DC

As of 2019 at least twenty states had passed or had pending legislation that specifically mentioned ACEs, including bills that provide funds for research and prevention of social problems that could be related to trauma experiences. In addition, the US government passed legislation in October 2018 called the Support for Patients and Communities Act, which recognizes that there are links between childhood trauma and substance abuse later in life. Under the law, a task force will provide recommendations

How Horses Helped Her Heal

On August 26, 2009, Jaycee Dugard was rescued after being held captive for eighteen years. At age eleven she had been walking to the school bus stop when she was abducted, thrown in the backseat of a car, and driven away. She was kept by her kidnappers inside their home, as well as outside in a confined area she calls "the backyard prison." After her rescue, Dugard needed an exceptional kind of treatment program that could help her heal from such severe trauma. What worked best for her was therapy with horses, also known as equine-facilitated therapy. "Horses have the special ability to make you be totally in the moment," says Dugard, "making talking about the trauma I went through so much easier and less painful."

Dugard made incredible progress in healing from her unimaginable trauma. She was then inspired to help others by founding the JAYC (Just Ask Yourself to Care) Foundation, which offers support, services, and professional referrals to trauma survivors and their families. "Trauma can shape you in many ways," she says. "One thing I know for sure, you have to face your fears to move beyond the pain. Finding a therapy program right for you is essential to moving forward. There are so many forms out there; for me, horse therapy resonated. The thing to remember is you can heal and you don't have to live with the nightmares forever."

Quoted in Nicola Bridges, "The Healing Power of Horses," *Parade*, February 17, 2019, pp. 10–11.

on how federal agencies can help families affected by trauma and substance abuse, and the US Department of Health and Human Services will teach educators and early childhood providers how to identify instances of trauma and how to address the problem. Also, schools may qualify for grants to implement new or improve existing trauma support services.

Trauma-Sensitive Schools

Of all the people who may observe signs of trauma in children, teachers are among the most likely. They see and work with their students day after day and often get to know them very well. Because of that, many educational groups and educators are seeing

> "Trauma-informed schools save lives."[66]
>
> —New York City teacher Laura DeInnocentiis

the value of trauma-sensitive, or trauma-informed, education. "Trauma-informed schools save lives," says New York City teacher Laura DeInnocentiis. She goes on to emphasize the important role educators can play in a traumatized student's life. "With an estimated one out of four children coming to school with a trauma history, teachers and staff need to become aware of the symptoms and educated in trauma-sensitive practice," says DeInnocentiis. "On average, students spend 35 hours a week with their teachers. This is a significant period of

Because teachers spend so much time with children, they get to know them well and are in a good position to spot signs of trauma.

time in which educators can positively impact the lives of their students."[66]

Matthew Portell, who is the principal at an elementary school in Nashville, Tennessee, implemented major changes to make his school trauma-informed. The school is located in a poor area of the city, and soon after becoming principal, Portell observed that many of the students showed signs of trauma. He knew that something had to be done to help these children, while also helping his teaching staff understand the effects of childhood trauma. "Our student behavior was nearly unmanageable, the teachers were physically and emotionally exhausted, and I was simply surviving," he says. Portell created a program that changed the school's culture, and the key part was changing how students were viewed and how teachers and administrators talked to them. "We had to stop asking, 'What is wrong with you?' to our students and start asking, 'What has happened to you?'"[67]

Within two years, the change was dramatic. Even though problems have not magically disappeared, the school environment is radically different from what he found when he first started working there. There were marked improvements in student behavior, and teachers no longer felt hopeless and burned out. "As the principal, I have been able to reflect on valuable lessons that a school should focus on when adopting a trauma-informed approach," he says. "Although the process is not easy, the benefits to students and staff outweigh the amount of effort needed."[68]

An Issue Worth Shouting About

Unlike scores of factors that are well known for harming people's health and well-being, the effects of childhood trauma have been known for only a little over two decades. But in that short amount of time, awareness has soared—as has a widespread

> "We need a national public campaign about toxic stress. We need to be shouting this from the rooftops."[69]
>
> —Nadine Burke Harris, a pediatrician and trauma expert who serves as California's surgeon general

sense of urgency that something must to be done to curb this problem. Many experts refer to childhood trauma as a matter of public health, which is as high a priority as other public health issues, such as an outbreak of infectious disease. One of those experts is Nadine Burke Harris, who emphatically calls it a public health crisis. "When you look at any successful public health campaign, it starts with raising awareness, so that people understand there is a problem to begin with," she says. "ACEs cross every line—racial, ethnic, geographic, gender, socio-economic. Today most parents are aware that secondhand smoke is really bad for kids, everyone has to wear a seatbelt, and lead is a neurotoxin. We need a national public campaign about toxic stress. We need to be shouting this from the rooftops."[69]

SOURCE NOTES

Introduction: Traumatized

1. Matthew Oransky, "Trauma: Our Nation's Hidden Public Health Crisis," *Teen Healthcare* (blog), Mount Sinai Adolescent Health Center, February 15, 2017. https://teenhealthcare.org.
2. Quoted in Dee Dee Chesley, "Toxic Stress Is a Public Health Crisis, Dr. Nadine Burke Harris Tells Erikson Audience," Erikson Institute, February 13, 2018. www.erikson.edu.
3. Quoted in Lauren Woods, "Become More Childhood Trauma Informed," UConn Today, April 9, 2018. https://today.uconn.edu.
4. Quoted in Anthony Pico, "Addressing Historical and Childhood Trauma: Why Native People Across the Country Are Gathering in San Diego in October," ACEs Connection, September 18, 2018. www.acesconnection.com.

Chapter One: A Public Health Emergency

5. Quoted in Mimi Kirk, "The Demographics of Childhood Trauma," *Pacific Standard*, February 22, 2018. https://psmag.com.
6. Bill Soules, "Teacher Discovers the Magnitude of Childhood Trauma," *Las Cruces (NM) Sun-News*, December 27, 2018. www.lcsun-news.com.
7. Soules, "Teacher Discovers the Magnitude of Childhood Trauma."
8. Soules, "Teacher Discovers the Magnitude of Childhood Trauma."
9. Vanessa Sacks and David Murphey, "The Prevalence of Adverse Childhood Experiences, Nationally, by State, and by Race or Ethnicity," Child Trends, February 20, 2018. www.childtrends.org.
10. Quoted in Kirk, "The Demographics of Childhood Trauma."

11. Renee Menart, "End Children's Trauma, Harm by Prioritizing Them When Parents Arrested, in Court," Juvenile Justice Information Exchange, December 5, 2018. https://jjie.org.
12. Quoted in Jeremy Loudenback, "A Teen's Guide to Healing from Parental Incarceration," *Chronicle of Social Change*, November 9, 2018. https://chronicleofsocialchange.org.
13. Quoted in Loudenback, "A Teen's Guide to Healing from Parental Incarceration."
14. Quoted in RAINN, "Survivor Story: Jeannette," March 22, 2016. www.rainn.org.
15. Quoted in RAINN, "Survivor Story."
16. Quoted in RAINN, "Survivor Story."
17. John Woodrow Cox and Steven Rich, "Scarred by School Shootings," *Washington Post*, March 25, 2018. www.washingtonpost.com.
18. Brooke Harrison, "Parkland Shooting Survivor Pens Personal Account, 'We Were Children That Came Out as Survivors of War,'" ABC News, March 23, 2018. https://abcnews.go.com.
19. Harrison, "Parkland Shooting Survivor Pens Personal Account, 'We Were Children That Came Out as Survivors of War.'"
20. Erika Christakis, "Active-Shooter Drills Are Tragically Misguided," *Atlantic*, March 2019. www.theatlantic.com.
21. Quoted in Steven Rich and John Woodrow Cox, "'What If Someone Was Shooting?'," *Washington Post*, December 26, 2018. www.washingtonpost.com.

Chapter Two: The Aftermath of Trauma

22. Laura DeInnocentiis, "The Story Behind the Student's Behavior: Trauma-Informed Schools Save Lives," *New York Parenting*, April 2018. www.nyparenting.com.
23. Quoted in Caitlin Reilly, "Lasting Damage: The Public Health Funder Linking Childhood Trauma and Illness," Inside Philanthropy, November 30, 2017. www.insidephilanthropy.com.

24. Quoted in Caroline Miller, “How Trauma Affects Kids in School,” Child Mind Institute, 2019. https://childmind.org.
25. Mona Delahooke, “When Adverse Childhood Experiences (ACEs) Underlie Problem Behaviors,” *Mona Delahooke, Ph.D* (blog), April 3, 2018. https://monadelahooke.com.
26. Quoted in Jennifer Dixon, “Toxic Stress of Poverty, Violence, Pain Alter Kids’ Brains,” *Detroit (MI) Free Press*, November 19, 2016. www.freep.com.
27. Center on the Developing Child, “Serve and Return,” 2019. https://developingchild.harvard.edu.
28. Quoted in Dixon, “Toxic Stress of Poverty, Violence, Pain Alter Kids’ Brains.”
29. Quoted in Alan Mozes, “Being Bullied May Alter the Teen Brain,” HealthDay, December 27, 2018. https://consumer.healthday.com.
30. Quoted in Tracey Bryant, “Bullying’s Lasting Harm,” University of Delaware, May 8, 2017. www.udel.edu.
31. Quoted in EurekAlert!, “Trauma in Childhood Linked to Drug Use in Adolescence,” June 8, 2016. www.eurekalert.org.
32. Quoted in Elisabet Kvarnstrom, “When Childhood Trauma Causes Addiction, Trauma-Focused Therapy Can Help Prevent Relapse,” Alta Mira Recovery Programs, May 10, 2018. www.altamirarecovery.com.
33. Quoted in Kvarnstrom, “When Childhood Trauma Causes Addiction, Trauma-Focused Therapy Can Help Prevent Relapse.”
34. Quoted in Elisabet Kvarnstrom, “Childhood Trauma and the Brain: How Therapy Can Restore Psychological Health After Sexual Abuse,” Bridges to Recovery, April 17, 2018. www.bridgestorecovery.com.
35. Quoted in Kvarnstrom, “Childhood Trauma and the Brain.”
36. Amy Smith, “Obituary: Nathan Houston Smith,” Dignity Memorial, August 15, 2018. www.dignitymemorial.com.
37. David Sack, “8 Reasons It’s So Hard to Overcome a Tough Childhood,” *Psychology Today*, May 12, 2015. www.psychologytoday.com.

Chapter Three: Harm That Can Last a Lifetime

38. Quoted in Joseph Brownstein, "Childhood Trauma May Shorten Life by 20 Years," ABC News, October 5, 2009. https://abcnews.go.com.
39. Quoted in Kristen Hovet, "Childhood Trauma: The Kids Are Not Alright and Part of the Explanation May Be Linked to Epigenetics," Genetic Literacy Project, November 14, 2017. https://geneticliteracyproject.org.
40. Shanta R. Dube, "How Childhood Trauma Can Affect Mental and Physical Health into Adulthood," Conversation, May 23, 2017. https://theconversation.com.
41. Quoted in Jane Ellen Stevens, "The Adverse Childhood Experiences Study—the Largest Public Health Study You Never Heard Of," Huffington Post, December 6, 2017. www.huffingtonpost.com.
42. Quoted in Brownstein, "Childhood Trauma May Shorten Life by 20 Years."
43. Elizabeth Hartney, "How Childhood Abuse Might Lead to Overeating," Verywell Mind, September 26, 2018. www.verywellmind.com.
44. Quoted in Salynn Boyles, "Abused Girls May Binge on Food as Adults," Everyday Health, May 30, 2013. www.everydayhealth.com.
45. Quoted in Maia Szalavitz, "If We Don't Focus on Why People Overeat, We Will Never Solve Obesity," *Guardian* (Manchester), September 27, 2017. www.theguardian.com.
46. Marc Gelkopf, "Social Injustice and the Cycle of Traumatic Childhood Experiences and Multiple Problems in Adulthood," JAMA Network, November 9, 2018. https://jamanetwork.com.
47. Quoted in William E. Copeland et al., "Association of Childhood Trauma Exposure with Adult Psychiatric Disorders and Functional Outcomes," JAMA Network, November 9, 2018. https://jamanetwork.com.

48. Quoted in Pat Anson, "Childhood Trauma Linked to Adult Pain," Pain News Network, May 11, 2018. www.painnews network.org.
49. Quoted in Anson, "Childhood Trauma Linked to Adult Pain."
50. Quoted in Sean Price, "What You Need to Know About ACEs," *Texas Medicine*, September 2017. www.texmed.org.
51. Quoted in Medical Xpress, "Parents Who Had Severe Trauma, Stresses in Childhood More Likely to Have Kids with Behavioral Health Problems," July 9, 2018. https://medicalxpress .com.
52. Quoted in Erin Blakemore, "Should Childhood Trauma Be Treated as a Public Health Crisis?," NPR, November 9, 2018. www.npr.org.

Chapter Four: The Dire Need for Solutions

53. Quoted in Harvard T.H. Chan School of Public Health, "Childhood Trauma's Devastating Impact on Health," 2015. www .hsph.harvard.edu.
54. Quoted in David Bornstein, "Opinion: Treating the Lifelong Harm of Childhood Trauma," *New York Times*, January 30, 2018. www.nytimes.com.
55. Quoted in Jayne O'Donnell, "'Toxic Stress' on Children Can Harm Their Lifelong Learning, Mental and Physical Health," *USA Today*, October 5, 2018. www.usatoday.com.
56. Quoted in Laurie Udesky, "Kaiser Family Medicine Clinic Launches 4-Question ACE Survey Pilot for Adults," ACEs Too High News, September 27, 2018. https://acestoohigh.com.
57. Ben Martin, "In-Depth: Cognitive Behavioral Therapy," PsychCentral, October 8, 2018. https://psychcentral.com.
58. Pamela Garber, "To Heal Trauma from Childhood, Relive the Neglect and Abuse," Aeon, December 24, 2015. https://aeon.co.
59. Garber, "To Heal Trauma from Childhood, Relive the Neglect and Abuse."

60. Alicia Armstrong, "Helping a Teen Boy Heal from Childhood Trauma with Virtual Reality," KVC Hospitals, November 14, 2018. https://hospitals.kvc.org.
61. Armstrong, "Helping a Teen Boy Heal from Childhood Trauma with Virtual Reality."
62. Armstrong, "Helping a Teen Boy Heal from Childhood Trauma with Virtual Reality."
63. Quoted in Mike Unger, "Monumental Effort," *Harvard Ed. Magazine*, Winter 2019. www.gse.harvard.edu.
64. Quoted in Unger, "Monumental Effort."
65. National Conference of State Legislatures, "Preventing and Mitigating the Effects of Adverse Childhood Experiences," *Health*, August 2018. www.ncsl.org.
66. DeInnocentiis, "The Story Behind the Student's Behavior."
67. Matthew Portell, "Making the Shift to a Trauma-Informed School," *Learning Is Social & Emotional* (blog), *Education Week*, July 24, 2018. https://blogs.edweek.org.
68. Portell, "Making the Shift to a Trauma-Informed School."
69. Quoted in Bornstein, "Opinion."

Center for Youth Wellness
3450 Third St.
Building 2, Suite 201
San Francisco, CA 94124
website: https://centerforyouthwellness.org

The Center for Youth Wellness seeks to advance pediatric medicine, raise public awareness, and transform the way society responds to children exposed to ACEs. The website offers news articles, information about the center's work, and a whole section on ACEs and toxic stress.

Child Mind Institute
101 E. Fifty-Sixth St.
New York, NY 10022
website: www.childmind.org

The Child Mind Institute is an independent nonprofit that seeks to transform the lives of children and families struggling with mental health and learning disorders. A wealth of information about childhood trauma is available through its website search engine.

Child Trauma Academy
1 Memorial City Plaza
800 Gessner Rd.
Houston, TX 77024
website: http://childtrauma.org

The Child Trauma Academy works to improve the lives of high-risk children through direct service, research, and education. Its website features a Child Trauma Library that offers a wealth of information about childhood trauma.

Futures Without Violence
100 Montgomery St., The Presidio
San Francisco, CA 94129
website: www.futureswithoutviolence.org

Futures Without Violence is a health and social justice organization that seeks to heal youth who have been traumatized by violence and to create healthy families and violence-free communities. Its website offers an extensive "Our Work" section with information about the organization's work, articles and publications, news releases, and other materials related to childhood trauma.

Look Through Their Eyes
Lurie Children's Hospital
Illinois Childhood Trauma Coalition
225 E. Chicago Ave., Box 10-B
Chicago, IL 60611
website: http://lookthroughtheireyes.org

A project of the Illinois Childhood Trauma Coalition, Look Through Their Eyes is devoted to helping people recognize childhood trauma by seeing through the eyes of children who are affected by it. Its website offers a wealth of statistics and other information for anyone wanting to better understand childhood trauma and what can be done about it.

National Child Traumatic Stress Network (NCTSN)
Center for Mental Health Services
Substance Abuse and Mental Health Services Administration
5600 Fishers Ln.
Parklawn Building, Room 17C-26
Rockville, MD 20857
website: www.nctsn.org

The NCTSN seeks to raise the standard of care and improve access to services for traumatized children, their families, and communities throughout the United States. The website features information about types of trauma, treatments for trauma, articles written especially for young people, and many other types of resources.

Trauma and Learning Policy Initiative (TLPI)
6 Everett St.
Cambridge, MA 02138
website: https://traumasensitiveschools.org

Through a number of advocacy strategies, the TLPI works to ensure that children traumatized by exposure to family violence and other ACEs succeed in school. Two sections of its website, “Trauma and Learning” and “Resources,” provide a wealth of information about childhood trauma and the role schools can play in helping traumatized kids.

Trauma Institute & Child Trauma Institute (TI & CTI)
85 Prospect St.
Northampton, MA 01060
website: www.childtrauma.com

The TI & CTI seeks to promote healing and healthy development of children, adolescents, and adults who have experienced trauma or loss. Its website offers information about childhood trauma, with most related to treatments and therapies.

Books

Ruth Gerson and Patrick Heppell, *Beyond PTSD: Helping and Healing Teens Exposed to Trauma*. Washington, DC: American Psychiatric Association, 2019.

Laurie Kahn, *Baffled by Love: Stories of the Lasting Impact of Childhood Trauma Inflicted by Loved Ones*. Berkeley, CA: She Writes, 2017.

Sheela Raja and Jaya Raja Ashrafi, *The PTSD Survival Guide for Teens*. Oakland, CA: New Harbinger, 2018.

Shannon Thomas, *Healing from Hidden Abuse: A Journey Through the Stages of Recovery from Psychological Abuse*. Tempe, AZ: MAST, 2016.

Mark Wolynn, *It Didn't Start with You: How Inherited Family Trauma Shapes Who We Are and How to End the Cycle*. New York: Viking, 2016.

Anyé Young, *Teen Guide to Living with Incarcerated Parents*. Pennsauken, NJ: BookBaby, 2018.

Internet Sources

Erin Blakemore, "Should Childhood Trauma Be Treated as a Public Health Crisis?," *Shots* (blog), NPR, November 9, 2018. www.npr.org.

Houston Behavioral Healthcare Hospital, "PTSD in Teens: Helping Adolescents Cope with Traumatic Events," May 30, 2018. www.houstonbehavioralhealth.com.

Matt Lavietes, "Children and PTSD: Health Risks Linger Long After Acute Psychological Trauma Ends," CNBC, July 13, 2018. www.cnbc.com.

Matthew Oransky, "Trauma: Our Nation's Hidden Public Health Crisis," *Teen Healthcare* (blog), Mount Sinai Adolescent Health Center, February 15, 2017. https://teenhealthcare.org.

Steven Rich and John Woodrow Cox, "How School Lockdowns Traumatize Children," *Washington Post*, December 26, 2018. www.washingtonpost.com.

INDEX

Note: Boldface page numbers indicate illustrations.

PICTURE CREDITS

Cover: eric1513/iStockphoto.com

7: Africa Studio/Shutterstock.com

12: Maury Aaseng

15: Brainsil/Shutterstock.com

19: Janos Rautonen/Shutterstock.com

25: Ridofranz/iStock.com

29: CLIPAREA l Custom media/Shutterstock.com

32: rez-art/Thinkstock.com

38: goodluz/Shutterstock.com

43: SeventyFour/Shutterstock.com

47: altanaka/Shutterstock.com

52: Rawpixel.com/Shutterstock.com

56: Lopolo/Shutterstock.com

60: wavebreakmedia/Shutterstock.com

ABOUT THE AUTHOR

Peggy J. Parks has written dozens of educational books on a wide variety of topics for children, teens, and young adults. She holds a bachelor's degree from Aquinas College in Grand Rapids, Michigan, where she graduated magna cum laude. Parks lives in Muskegon, Michigan, a town she says inspires her writing because of its location on the shores of beautiful Lake Michigan.